*John Burningham*

# MOUSE HOUSE

CANDLEWICK PRESS

For Lily

First U.S. edition 2018

Originally published in Great Britain by Jonathan Cape,
an imprint of Random House Children's Publishers UK,
a Penguin Random House Company

Library of Congress Catalog Card Number pending
ISBN 978-1-5362-0039-3

18 19 20 21 22 23 TLF 10 9 8 7 6 5 4 3 2 1

Printed in Dongguan, Guangdong, China

This book was typeset in Goudy Old Style.

Candlewick Press
99 Dover Street
Somerville, Massachusetts 02144

visit us at www.candlewick.com

This is the house . . .

where the family lives.
Every evening, they have their supper
and then the children go to bed.

But there is another family living in the house.
Do you know who they are?

They are the mouse family.

After the humans have gone to bed,
the mice look for food.

Then the mice have their supper.
Afterward, the mouse children start to play.

The father phones the mouse catcher.
"The mouse catcher will be here in the morning
to get rid of the mice."

"Why do we have to get rid of the mice?"
ask the children.
"They don't do any harm."

"They will be all over the house if we don't," says the father. "We must get rid of them." Before they go to bed, the children write a message to the mice.

To the mouse family

your lives are in danger

you must get out of the house tonight

from the children

"I hear you have a problem with mice,"
the mouse catcher says.

"I've come to deal
with them.

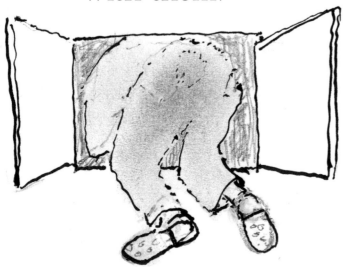

They get
everywhere.

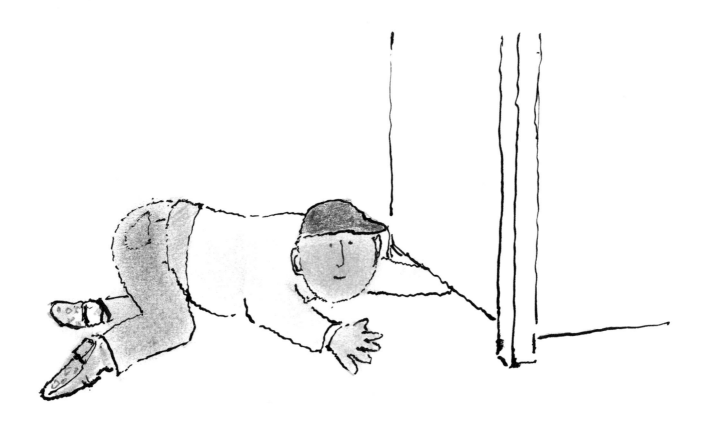

You won't have any
more mice once they have
eaten my little packets.

In a few days, you will be mouse-free."

From their bedroom
window, the children
can see the mice
playing outside
at night.

They decide to make things
for the mice to play on.

They make a trampoline,

a slide, and a swing.

And they watch the mouse children
playing in the evenings.

In autumn, the leaves start to fall.
Soon it will be winter.

After it snows, all the mouse toys are gone.
No swings. No slide. No trampoline.
"They didn't even leave a note for us,"
says the little girl.

But, in time, the children forget
about the mice and play their own games.

One night, the boy is on his way to bed
when he sees a mouse.

But he doesn't say anything at all.